SHARE THE FEAR!

You are not alone. And I don't mean that a creature lurks in the dark shadows of your bedroom. Or a slimy menace lives under your bed. (Although that might be true.) I mean, you are not alone in being afraid. Everyone is afraid of something. Every. Single. Person. Reading about other people's fears in these weird tales, you might learn how to overcome your own. Or you might learn how to escape from zombie teachers attacking the school. Both are good things to know. Just make sure you leave the lights on while reading!

CONTENTS

Chapter 1

GNOME IS WHERE THE HEART IS

Pitter-patter, pitter-patter, the words in Stan's book read. *Mason peeked round a corner. He saw the top of a pointy hat, about waist-high, and he knew this was the end. After all he'd done to get away, the gnome had finally found him.*

Stan swallowed and burrowed deeper under his covers. He wasn't supposed to read scary stories before bed. But he'd found a book of scary stories about gnomes – creepy gnomes had always scared him silly – and he couldn't resist. The main character was even eleven, like he was.

Mason took a deep breath. His only chance was to run fast and hope the gnome wouldn't hear him. He checked to make sure the pointy hat was still there, and then he took off.

Stan held his breath, feeling almost like he was running with Mason. He turned the page and shifted in bed. His torch wobbled.

Mason sprinted down the hall. His ears searched for any sound of the gnome – but so far, he heard nothing. His heart sang – he was home free! He saw the end of the hallway where the front door was.

And suddenly, the gnome stepped in front of it.

Stan's heart stopped for a moment. He rolled over in his bed and felt something sharp. Without meaning to, he let out a yelp and grabbed what was poking him. When he brought it up to his face, he screamed.

It was a gnome. A small, plastic one, anyway.

Stan threw the gnome and scrambled to sit up. Just then the ceiling light in his room turned on. His mum stood in the doorway, panting.

"Stan!" Mum said, strands of hair sticking out of her ponytail. "What is going on?"

"Uh . . . ," Stan said. He really didn't want to admit that a toy garden gnome had made him scream. But then he heard a familiar sound – his older sister, Margie, cackling.

Stan knew exactly who had put the gnome in his bed.

Margie stuck her head in the room from the other side of the door frame.

"He was screaming about a toy, Mum," she said, grinning. Her eyes narrowed into the mean look Stan knew very well.

"I rolled over and it almost punctured my kidney!" he said, sitting up and sliding his book and torch under his covers so his mum wouldn't notice.

Margie snorted, and Mum gave Stan "The Look". "I don't think rolling over onto a toy could puncture your kidney, Stan," Mum said. "Unless your toy is a steak knife. Why is a toy in your bed, anyway? You should be sleeping."

"It's not *my* toy. It's Margie's," Stan said, pointing to the gnome lying on the floor. "She knows I hate gnomes and she put it in my bed to be mean!"

Margie tried to hide a laugh, but now their mum gave *her* "The Look". She threw her hands up.

"What kind of person is afraid of a garden ornament?" Margie asked. "I'm just doing him a *favour*. If he gets used to them, maybe he wouldn't be embarrassed to make more friends other than Artie."

"It's not just any garden ornament," Stan mumbled. But he still felt embarrassed. He didn't know why, but garden gnomes had always freaked him out. And his sister never let him forget it.

While Stan was thinking about his fear, Margie stepped into his room and threw back his covers before he could stop her.

"If you're so scared of gnomes, why are you reading a book about them?" she said, grinning.

His book had closed and the cover sat exposed. *Gnome Is Where the Heart Is,* it read. His torch rolled off the bed and landed on the floor, spotlighting the toy gnome.

Stan's mother sighed. "Honey . . . I'm not sure why you're afraid of gnomes either. But I'm *really* not sure why you'd read a scary book about them. Especially before bed." She swept up the book and pointed to the torch and the toy on the floor. Margie grabbed those, grinning at him the whole time. Stan stuck his tongue out at her when his mum wasn't looking.

"Now go to sleep," Mum said, turning off the light. She and Margie left Stan alone in the dark.

Stan was pretty sure he wouldn't get to sleep. He wished he knew why he didn't like gnomes. He wished he didn't feel so weird about it. And his sister wasn't wrong. Stan didn't like to make friends, because then he'd have to tell them about his fears. But now wasn't the time to think about that.

Stan tried to dream of normal things like football and his friends and climbing trees. But the minute he closed his eyes, the nightmare gnomes were waiting for him.

Chapter 2

THE GNOMELY COTTAGE

In the morning, Stan's dad shouted to him from the kitchen. Stan came downstairs. His dad stood over the cooker, making eggs. The newsreader on TV droned on behind him.

"Hey, bud," Dad said. "It's just you and me for breakfast today. Mum went to work early and Margie is at a friend's. Sit down and grab some pancakes."

Stan didn't have to be told twice. He jumped on a chair and slid up to the table. As soon as his dad put the pancakes in front of him, he dug in.

On the news, the newsreader said, "A forty-three-year-old woman living in the Neary Heights area has been reported missing. This is the third missing person in the neighbourhood in two months."

Dad made a clicking noise with his tongue. "That's not good," he said.

Stan's phone buzzed in his pocket, and he checked it while his dad looked at the news. It was a text from Artie: *Want to come over to mine tonight?*

Stan grinned and swallowed his bite. "Dad, can I spend the night at Artie's?"

Dad was still watching TV, so it took him a minute or so to respond. "I don't know, Stan.

I don't like this missing person stuff."

Stan sat up straight. "I'll walk straight there and text you when I arrive. It's only just down the road." He crossed his fingers, hoping for permission. School had just finished for the summer. He wanted to start his holidays off right – hanging out with his best friend.

Dad thought about it for a minute. "Okay. But walk *straight* there. And text me and Mum the instant you get there."

Stan didn't bother to hide his fist pump. Dad grinned. Stan put his plate on the worktop and sprinted up to his room. He texted Artie: *Dad said yes!*

Stan looked round for his lucky cap and then had a thought. He texted Artie again: *But only if you take that garden gnome out of ur garden before I come over.*

There was a pause, and then Artie wrote back: *Are u serious?*

Stan saw his cap sticking out from under his bed and grabbed it. Then he texted firmly: *Yes.*

Artie wrote back: *OK. Good thing ur my best friend. Otherwise I would think ur weird.*

Stan grinned and fist-pumped again. This was shaping up to be a great start to the summer.

* * *

At Artie's, Stan noticed the gnome was gone. He breathed a sigh of relief and texted his parents to tell them he'd got to Artie's okay. Artie dragged Stan inside and made him drop off his stuff.

"We're going out!" Artie said to his

sixteen-year-old sister, who sat on the sofa flipping through a magazine. Artie's sister didn't even look up. She reminded Stan of his own older sister.

"Whatever," she said. "Be back by dark. Mum and Dad have plans after work. They are going to be home late."

Artie grinned and pulled Stan out the door again. "I have to show you something. In the woods. Come on!"

Stan laughed and tried to keep up with Artie as they raced to the woods near Artie's house. Neary Heights backed onto a nature reserve. Artie and Stan had recently talked their parents into letting them explore the woods there.

The two friends skimmed over the forest floor and through the sun-streaked trees. Artie took a path they hadn't explored before.

Stan felt a pang of nervousness, but he swallowed it down. Finally, they crashed through some bushes and landed in a little clearing.

Stan stopped and caught his breath while Artie stood next to him, beaming.

"Look!" Artie said, sweeping his arm through the clearing. Stan followed his arm to where he was pointing. It was a cottage – a lonely, rundown cottage sitting in the middle of the forest.

Stan grinned. A fort. A pre-built fort where they could hide out whenever.

"This is *awesome*, Artie!" he said.

Artie grinned back. "Come inside. It's so *creepy*," he said, his eyes twinkling. Stan followed him to the cottage, up the creaky steps, and through a door that squeaked loudly as they swung it open.

The inside of the cottage looked as bad as the outside. Near the front, its small kitchen had dangling, decayed cupboards and a caved-in sink. Towards the back, they found several small rooms. All of them were full of rotting wood and sagging floors.

Artie and Stan returned to the front of the cottage and Artie closed the door.

"This is the best part," Artie said. He flipped a bolt lock on the door.

Stan's eyes widened. "The lock actually works?" he said.

"Yep," Artie said. "Our own secret hideaway – no one can get in once we lock it." They grinned at each other.

Then Stan heard something pattering outside around the cottage. It sounded like little feet running back and forth. He shook his head – he had to be imagining things. The cottage was a little spooky. But it was really exciting too.

"Let's look around," Stan said. "Hey, look! Old tennis rackets." Stan threw one to Artie and they grinned. Stan couldn't wait to see what else they would find.

The friends played all day. Every once in a while, Stan thought he heard little footsteps outside, but it had to be just the leaves rustling or something. Nothing else would make sense. As the sun started to set, Artie and Stan headed home.

The streets were bathed in shadows as they walked back to Artie's house. Stan looked around at all the front lawns. There seemed to be an alarming number of garden gnomes on them. Way more than he'd ever noticed before. He shivered.

"Is it just me, or are there more gnomes in

this street?" Stan asked as they neared Artie's house. Artie rolled his eyes.

"You have gnomes on the brain," he said.

"No, I'm serious," Stan said. "There are clumps of them everywhere." Sure enough, five gnomes stood in a circle on the front lawn next to Artie's house.

Artie huffed. "You have to get over it, Stan. They're just garden ornaments."

Just as the sky turned a deep blue and the sun set completely, they reached Artie's house and went in.

Artie's sister had heated up some spaghetti and the whole house smelled delicious. She put plates of pasta on the table when they got in. She pointed to the dishes and said, "Here. Dinner." Then she went back to her phone.

Artie made a face at his sister behind her back and Stan giggled. But when she turned around the two of them had started eating their spaghetti, innocent looks pasted on their faces. She frowned at them but then turned back to her phone.

Stan and Artie tried to keep from laughing. It didn't work – they laughed all through dinner, getting spaghetti sauce everywhere.

After they ate, they were both pretty tired, but no way were they planning on going to sleep straight away.

"Film?" Artie asked.

"That's a great idea!" Stan said. "A scary one, maybe?"

"Unless it's got gnomes in it," Artie grumbled.

Stan rolled his eyes. "I don't know why it bothers you. Get over it!"

Artie ignored that and grabbed his

sleeping bag and put it in front of the TV. Stan did the same and then went into the bathroom to brush his teeth.

When Stan came out, he saw Artie snuggled in his sleeping bag. But Artie's bag moved with what looked like laughter. Stan came all the way round the sofa and froze.

There, in Stan's sleeping bag, was Artie's garden gnome – all tucked in.

Chapter 3

A GNOME RUN

"Come on, Stan, it was just a joke!" Artie's voice called behind him. Stan didn't even look back. Some friend he was. He pulled his overnight bag closer and stomped down Artie's street.

"Your dad is going to be so annoyed, Stan. It's dark outside! Just wait till my parents get home." Artie's words rang out.

Stan paused but then kept walking. He turned the corner. He knew Artie was right.

It didn't matter. He'd rather walk the two dark streets to his house than spend another minute with a friend who had betrayed him.

After a couple of minutes, Stan calmed down. He looked round for the first time since he'd stormed out of Artie's house. The night was unusually cool, and Stan could see the ghost of his breath when he breathed out.

The street was full of shadows, and the moon hid behind clouds. A street light above Stan flickered and then went out. Suddenly, as he stood on the dark pavement looking down the dark street, he wasn't so sure it was a good idea he'd taken off. But he was already halfway home, so he didn't really have a choice now.

Stan walked faster. He clung to his bag, holding it like a shield in front of him. An owl hooted somewhere, making him jump.

But then he heard a sound that made his blood run cold. The pitter-patter was back, just as it had been by the cottage. It sounded as if it came from between the houses.

Pitter-patter, pitter-patter, pitter-patter, pitter-patter.

This time it sounded as if it was right behind him.

Stan whirled round, breathing hard, ready to throw his bag at whatever was behind him. But when he looked, there was nothing. He turned back around.

Pitter-patter, pitter-patter, pitter-patter, pitter-patter.

Laughter echoed off the houses all along the street. Stan looked around wildly. The pitter-pats got louder – now it sounded as if a stadium full of monsters was after him. Stan didn't wait to see if he was right. He threw his

bag down and sprinted towards his house.

The laughter got louder. Something shifted in the shadows behind the trees on the front lawns. Something moved fast and seemed to be gaining on Stan.

Stan saw his house and its warm, comforting lights five houses away. He was sure he wouldn't make it. The laughter swirled all around him now. The footsteps sounded like big creatures coming to take him down. Four houses, three houses, two houses . . .

* * *

Stan sprinted up his drive and threw himself against the door.

Locked.

He rang the doorbell over and over and

over again. Finally his mum opened the door.

"Stan!" Mum said, her eyebrows raised with worry. Stan pushed past her. Then he slammed the door closed and locked it tight. He looked out the side window to see what had been chasing him.

Nothing looked back. Just the dark street and the neighbours' houses, lined up neatly.

"*What* are you doing?" Mum asked. "Are you okay?"

Stan turned around and wiped the sweat off his forehead. He suddenly felt like a big baby, scared of his own shadow. "Yeah, I'm okay. Just thought I'd come home for the night!" he said brightly.

Mum put her hands on her hips and stared at him.

* * *

Stan didn't sleep well that night. So when the doorbell rang early in the morning, he was already cranky. But when he heard Artie's voice talking to his dad, he got crankier.

"STAN!" his dad called up the stairs. "Artie's here. Come down."

Stan stood at the top of the stairs, looking down, hoping Artie wouldn't look up. But sure enough, Artie looked up and spotted him. Now Stan *had* to go down. He sighed and trudged down the stairs.

Artie stood by the door sheepishly. "Hey, Stan," he said.

Stan stood in front of him and crossed his arms. He didn't say anything.

Artie cleared his throat. "Okay, I'm really, really sorry about last night. I shouldn't have stuck that gnome in there."

Stan didn't feel better. "You thought it was funny."

Artie shrugged. "It's just really hard to understand why you're so scared of them. Though I did notice that there *are* more gnomes around here than before. I think you're right."

Stan didn't believe Artie. He was just saying that to try and make peace. And Stan wasn't interested.

"Do you want to hang out?" Artie asked.

"I'm busy," Stan said. Then he turned his back on his best friend and went back up the stairs. He leaned against the wall. Tears stung his eyes. He just wasn't ready to forgive Artie. He swallowed down his sadness and let it turn to anger.

After a moment, Stan heard the front door

open and then close. He went back to his
room and started playing a video game.
But his heart wasn't in it. After a little while,
he heard a knock on his bedroom door.

Dad came in and sat down beside him.
"That was pretty harsh, Stan. Don't you think
you could have forgiven Artie?" he said.

Stan shrugged. He did feel bad. But he
wasn't about to let his dad know. Or Artie.

"Well," Dad said in his "don't argue"
voice, "you're not going to sit in here playing
video games all day. Go outside. But stay in
the garden. You can try that rocket launcher
on the front lawn."

Stan brightened up a little and switched
off his video game. That wasn't so bad. The
rocket launcher would have been more fun
with Artie, but it could still be fun.

His dad tousled his hair, and Stan grabbed

the launcher and went outside.

On the front lawn, Stan set up his rocket launcher and reread the directions. The wind picked up and blew the paper out of his hands – right into his neighbour's lawn.

The paper landed and wrapped around a garden gnome standing on their lawn.

Stan went still. He didn't remember the neighbours having a gnome before. But he needed those directions if he wanted to launch the rocket. Still, the thought of touching that gnome . . .

Stan squared his shoulders. Maybe this was exactly the time he would get over his fear. He took a deep breath and walked slowly over to his neighbour's gnome. The paper had wrapped around the gnome's face and part of his pointy hat. Stan inched closer.

Just a lawn ornament, Stan thought. *A thing people put in their garden that doesn't move.*

He swallowed and reached out his arm slowly. He peeled off the paper and then jumped back.

The gnome's face was frozen in a scream.

Chapter 4

GNOMEBODY BELIEVES ME

Stan stumbled backwards. He scrambled to his house just as his mum's car pulled into the driveway. He didn't wait to talk to her outside. He ran inside, where his dad was on the floor working on a plug socket.

Stan felt weirdly triumphant about the gnome next door. He was *sure* that's not what a typical lawn ornament looked like. And now he could show people. Something was up with the neighbourhood gnomes in Neary Heights. His mum walked into the house just as his sister stomped down the stairs.

"Dad, what's for dinner?" she yelled.

"I'm right here, Margie," Dad said. "There's no need to shout. Tacos."

"Yummm," Mum said. Dad stood up and went to give her a kiss.

"Guys," Stan said breathlessly. "I have to show you something." He didn't have time for tacos.

His mum's phone buzzed, but she ignored it. "I'm off work," she said, almost to herself.

"What is it, bud?" Dad asked Stan. But just as Stan opened his mouth, his dad's phone buzzed too.

His parents shared a look. "That's weird. Maybe it's something important?" Mum said.

She checked her phone. "It's Artie's parents." Mum dialled her voicemail and started listening to the message.

"I just need to tell you –" Stan started to say, but his mum raised her finger as she listened. Her eyes widened.

"Is Artie here, Stan?" she asked.

Stan shook his head. Mum pressed another button on the phone and put it to her ear.

"Carmela," she said, using Artie's mum's first name, "we'll be right there." She put the phone down and looked at Dad.

"It's Artie," she said. "He's gone missing."

Stan felt something like icy water trickle down his back. His best friend missing? That just couldn't be.

"He's just playing a trick," Stan said, his voice wobbling. "Mum, you have to go and look at the gnome next door. It's important."

She sighed. "Now is not the time, Stan. Margie, you're in charge. Dad and I are going to go and help search for Artie." Margie nodded, but then made a face at Stan behind their parents' backs.

Mum and Dad moved fast, grabbing keys and torches and jackets before heading out the door. After they'd gone, Margie said, "Grab your own tacos. I'll be in my room."

Stan felt frustrated and worried. He had been so mean to Artie . . . and there was that gnome next door too.

Stan sat down at the dining room table next to the sliding glass door. As he thought about what he should do next, he looked at his reflection. Just beyond his image, he could see the outlines of trees outside in the dark.

And then Stan saw something move in the dark. He stood up and moved closer to the glass door. As he did, he heard a familiar sound that sent shivers down his spine.

Pitter-patter, pitter-patter, pitter-patter, pitter-patter.

Stan didn't wait to see what it was. He sprinted up to Margie's room and flung open her door. She was lying on her bed talking to someone on speakerphone.

"MARGIE!" Stan yelled. "There's something outside."

Margie stopped talking long enough to roll her eyes at him. "Yeah. Like nature," she said.

"No, I'm telling you, someone is running around our house!"

"I'll call you back," Margie said to her phone. "My little brother is freaking out about something. Again." She pressed a button and looked at Stan. "I was *talking* to someone, Stan."

"I know. But outside the window, I saw something move and I heard this noise . . ." Stan was talking way too fast, but he couldn't stop. "And earlier today, I saw this gnome who was screaming –"

"Really, STAN? Not the gnomes again. Get out of my room. Stop being such a wimp!" She put in her earbuds and pressed buttons on her phone. "Hey, Annabel? Sorry. My brother is so weird."

"Arrrgh," Stan said. "You are such a mean sister!" He slammed the door shut and hoped a gnome would get her.

Chapter 5

A GNOME AGAIN, NATURALLY

Stan paced around the living room, thinking about Artie and how mean he'd been to him. Thinking about how mean his sister was being to him. And thinking about, as always, lately – garden gnomes.

He wasn't quite sure what to do with himself. He ran to the dining room and shut the curtains to the sliding glass door. Then he

closed the blinds all around the house.
The less he saw, the better.

Stan turned on the TV and the news
popped up. Before he could get to another
channel, the newsreader caught his attention.

"Neary Heights is the newest
neighbourhood going through a missing
persons epidemic. In one day, more than
fifteen men, women and children have been
reported missing."

The cameraman panned around the street
and Stan jumped. That was Artie's street. As
the camera scanned the lawns, Stan's blood
ran cold. Gnomes were everywhere. On
every lawn, by every tree and even on the
pavement – gnomes had taken over.

Stan turned off the TV, his heart racing.
That was Artie's street. And Artie was gone.
He had to find him. He had to make up for

how mean he'd been. But where could Artie have gone?

Stan sat up straight.

The cottage. Of course! Artie would have gone to the cottage.

For a minute, Stan didn't think he could find the courage. The gnomes, the woods, everything . . . it was all too scary. But then he thought about Artie's face when he'd basically told him to go away. And he knew he had to find him.

Stan grabbed his jacket and a torch. The sun had long since set, and he'd be going through the woods. Without saying anything to his sister, he slipped out the door into the cool night.

The first thing Stan did was look at his neighbour's front lawn to see the gnome with the scream-face. But he couldn't find him –

only because there were at least twelve more gnomes there now. And they were all facing the screaming gnome – standing in rows like an army.

Stan shivered. He turned away from them slowly and began walking towards the woods. A bead of sweat formed on his temple and trickled down his face. He refused to look back at the gnomes.

But then he heard it.

Pitter-patter, pitter-patter.

Stan swung around, expecting to find nothing yet again. But what he saw stopped him cold.

The twelve gnomes around the screaming gnome had moved. They were closer now. And they had all turned to face Stan.

Pitter-patter, pitter-patter, pitter-patter, pitter-patter.

Stan could sense other gnomes encircling him. He had to get to the woods. He spun round and ran off.

PITTER-PATTER, PITTER-PATTER, PITTER-PATTER, PITPATPITPATPITPAT.

Stan didn't need to turn round to know the gnomes were following him. On his left and right, gnomes from the houses began running alongside him. Soon he was being chased by an entire mob. He sped up and hit the forest at a breakneck pace, trying not to panic.

All around him, crashing and laughing sounds came from every part of the forest. Stan swtiched on his torch to light the way ahead. Finally, he caught the outline of the cottage and sprinted even faster.

Chapter 6

FEELING GNOMESICK

Stan jumped over branches and raced across the soft forest floor. He felt the whooshes of little bodies running beside him. Something grabbed at his trousers, and Stan brushed at it in a panic. Other things grabbed at him and flailed wildly. He was so close to the cottage he could almost smell it. He finally made it and ran up the creaky stairs.

He slammed through the door and locked it behind him just in time.

Stan leaned his back against the door, trying to catch his breath. He heard *PITTER-PATTER, PITTER-PATTER* all around him now. High whines of laughter echoed off the trees. When he looked out of the window, his heart stopped.

Stan was surrounded. Gnomes were everywhere, running and jumping and clawing at the cottage. A gnome jumped up to the window, and Stan screamed and backed up. He crawled to a wall in the cottage and tried to think.

"Artie?" Stan called out. "Are you here?" But the only answer was the *WHACK, WHACK, WHACK* sounds of gnomes hitting the sides of the cottage.

But then he heard a low moan.

Stan stood up. That could be Artie! He ran from room to room in the cottage, shining his torch and searching frantically. Nothing.

"Artie?" he called. "Artie, are you in here?"

The low moan happened again, but Stan couldn't place where it was coming from. Then something even stranger happened – the pitter-patter, the laughter and the thumping completely stopped. For a moment, the cottage was wrapped in complete silence.

Then the low moan sounded again. It was outside the window, near the front door. Carefully, Stan dropped to his knees and crawled across the dirty floor. He peeked over the edge of the windowsill. Just below him stood a small figure.

Stan pointed his torch at the figure. It was a gnome. Its back was turned, and it was letting out a low, scary moan. Then, ever so slowly – right before his eyes – the gnome turned around and looked up.

Stan gasped and dropped his torch.

The gnome looked exactly like Artie. And its mouth was frozen in a terrifying scream.

Chapter 7

DRIVING THIS GNOME

Stan scrambled to his torch and picked it up with shaking hands. Artie-the-Gnome moaned again, but this time the other gnomes joined him.

Stan stood up and pointed the torch out of the window. His knees buckled. Dozens – maybe hundreds – of gnomes stood staring at the cottage. All of them were swaying and moaning. Worse, he could now recognize them.

Some of them were neighbours. Some were people he recognized on the news. All of them were after him.

Stan couldn't move.

He had to get back to his own house. The cottage wouldn't hold up much longer, and he needed to make sure his family was okay. Stan turned around, looking for something, anything, to help. Then his hand brushed against something leaning against the wall.

The old tennis rackets.

Stan picked them both up. He didn't want to hurt the gnomes – they were his neighbours and Artie, after all. But he might be able to get them to move out of his way. He just needed a clear path to his home.

Stan squared his shoulders and opened the door. Holding a racket in each hand, he walked slowly down the rickety stairs.

The gnomes swayed and moaned, turning in sync with him as he walked out. Artie's little gnome body swivelled around completely as Stan walked by.

"Sorry, Artie. I'm going to find a way to fix this," Stan whispered.

Stan walked faster and faster, and the moaning grew louder. Finally, Stan couldn't take it any more, and he started running.

From behind him, Stan heard a shriek and then the *pitter-patter* sound of feet he dreaded. He started swinging the rackets.

Back and forth, back and forth, Stan whooshed the rackets in front and behind. While his swings slowed his running, they created a force field of movement that none of the gnomes could get through. And for a minute, Stan rejoiced. Maybe he could make it out of this forest after all!

Up ahead of him, Stan spotted his own street and picked up the pace. As he ran faster, he stopped swinging the tennis rackets. That's when he noticed something strange.

The gnomes were gone.

Just like that.

There was no sign of them.

Stan reached the street and stopped for a second to catch his breath. He peered back into the forest from the pavement. Nothing. No gnomes, no pitter-patter, no laughter. Perhaps his tennis rackets had completely scared them away.

Stan slowed his breathing and turned around, looking at the ground as he pondered his next move. He had to go home and get his family. His mum and dad would know what to do. He looked up and took a step forward.

"Ahh!" Stan gasped. Right in front of him

stood Artie-the-Gnome. Artie looked up at him and moaned. Then, before Stan could do anything, Artie reached up and touched him.

And the world went black.

Chapter 8

WHEN IN GNOME

Stan slowly woke up, the darkness over his vision gradually clearing. He had no idea how long he had been out of it. Or where Artie was now. Somehow, the night had completely vanished, and it was daylight now. But something was wrong. He felt as if he was standing up, but he couldn't be. He was way too short.

What's more, Stan seemed to be in his own front lawn, looking at the door to his house. His back felt scratchy because of the tree he leaned against. But even worse, he felt like he *had* to do something. And he was so hungry. But not for food. For something . . . else.

A car pulled up in his driveway and his parents jumped out. He tried to yell for them, but all that came out was a low moan. At the same time, his sister burst out of the house in tears.

"I can't find Stan anywhere!" she yelled, before her parents could say anything.

Stan tried to talk again, but he could still only manage a moan. The strange itch – the hunger – had got stronger too.

"Stay here, Margie," Dad said. "We're going to search for him."

"And call the police!" Mum yelled as she and his dad hopped back in the car and peeled out of the driveway.

Margie. Stan felt the itch grow. It grew so much, he suddenly could move. He turned his head and watched his sister. As she moved towards the house, he understood what it was he wanted.

He wanted – no, needed – his sister to become just like him.

Pitter-patter, pitter-patter.

Stan ran towards her, reaching out and moaning all the way.

ABOUT THE AUTHOR

Megan Atwood is a writer and professor with more than 45 books published. She lives in New Jersey, USA, where she wrangles cats, dreams up scary stories and thinks of ways to keep kids on the edge of their seats.

ABOUT THE ILLUSTRATOR

Neil Evans is a Welsh illustrator. A life-long comic art fan, he drifted into children's illustration at art college and has since done plenty of both. He enjoyed a few years as a member of various unheard-of indie rock bands (and as a maker of bizarre small press comics) before settling down to get serious about making a living from illustration. He loves depicting emotion, expression and body language, and he loves inventing unusual creatures and places. When not hunched over a graphics tablet, he can usually be found hunched over a guitar, or dreaming up book pitches and silly songs with his partner, Susannah. They live together in North Wales.

GLOSSARY

decayed broken down or rotten

epidemic sudden, widespread occurrence of an undesirable phenomenon, such as an outbreak of disease or violent crime

frustrated helpless or discouraged

gnome dwarf-like old man from folklore and fairy tales

kidney organ that filters waste products from the blood and turns them into urine

pang sudden, brief pain or emotion

reserve place where animals and plants can live and be protected from harm or damage

swivel turn or rotate on the spot

tousle mess up someone's hair

TALK ABOUT IT

1. Stan is caught reading a scary book about garden gnomes at the beginning of the story. Why do you think he would read about gnomes if he is terrified by them?

2. Artie plays a prank on Stan by placing a garden gnome in his sleeping bag. Share a time someone played a prank on you. How did it make you feel?

3. When the gnomes surround Stan in the cottage, he grabs the tennis rackets and makes a run for it. What would you have done in his situation instead?

WRITE ABOUT IT

1. What is the creepiest or scariest lawn ornament you've ever seen in someone's garden? Draw a picture of it and write a paragraph explaining why it was so scary. If you haven't seen one, imagine what one would look like.

2. We don't get to see how Artie was turned into a gnome. Write a new scene that describes how it happened.

3. At the end of the story, Stan becomes a garden gnome and chases after his sister. Write a new chapter to shows what happens next. Does he change her into a gnome too or does he somehow turn back to normal? You decide!